Pepys and his Contemporaries

Richard Ollard

Published in Great Britain by National Portrait Gallery Publications,
National Portrait Gallery, St Martin's Place, London WC2H 0HE

For a complete catalogue of current publications please write to the
address above, or visit our website at www.npg.org.uk/publications

First published 2000
This edition published 2015

This edition retains Richard Ollard's original text with new additions
by Catharine MacLeod, Curator of Seventeenth-Century Portraits at the
National Portrait Gallery, London, as indicated (*) in the list of contents.

Extracts from *The Diary of Samuel Pepys Vol. 1–9* edited by Robert Latham
& W. Matthews reprinted by permission of Peters Fraser & Dunlop
(www.petersfraserdunlop.com) on behalf of the Estate of Robert Latham.

ISBN 978 1 85514 585 6

A catalogue record for this book is available from the British Library.

Managing Editor: Christopher Tinker
Editors: Susie Foster, Andrew Roff
Design: Smith & Gilmour
Production: Ruth Müller-Wirth, Kathleen Bloomfield
Printed and bound in China

The publisher would like to thank the copyright holders for granting
permission to reproduce works illustrated in this book. Every effort
has been made to contact the holders of copyright material, and
any omissions will be corrected in future editions if the publisher
is notified in writing.

Contents

* Additional entries and 'Pepys and the Restoration Art World' by Catharine MacLeod, Curator of Seventeenth-Century Portraits at the National Portrait Gallery, London

OPPOSITE
Samuel Pepys
John Hales, 1666
The gown worn by Pepys was hired especially for this portrait, and the music he holds is his own composition, a setting of a poem by William Davenant, 'Beauty, Retire'.

PEPYS ON SITTING FOR HIS PORTRAIT BY JOHN HALES

The Diary, Vol. 7, 17 March 1666

... At noon home to dinner, and presently with my wife out to Hales's, where I am still infinitely pleased with my wife's picture. I paid him 14l for it, and 25s for the frame, and I think it not a whit too dear for so good a picture. It is not yet quite finished and dry, so as to be fit to bring home yet. This day I begun to sit, and he will make me, I think, a very fine picture. He promises it shall be as good as my wife's, and I sit to have it full of shadows, and do almost break my neck looking over my shoulder to make the posture for him to work by.

OPPOSITE
Diary extract from 17 March 1666 (with transcription above)

March.

[illegible]
[illegible] Sir W. B. [illegible]
[illegible] Whitehall [illegible]
[illegible] Boy [illegible]
[illegible] 12 [illegible]
[illegible] Journall [illegible]
[illegible] scratched [illegible]
[illegible]
[illegible] Idle [illegible]
17 [illegible] Journall [illegible]
[illegible]
[illegible] Hales's [illegible]
[illegible] 14 [illegible] 25 [illegible]
[illegible]
[illegible]
[illegible]
[illegible]
[illegible]
[illegible] Barbary
[illegible]
[illegible] W. Hewers [illegible]
[illegible] ale [illegible]
[illegible] Sir W. B. [illegible] Lord Middleton
[illegible]
[illegible]
[illegible]
[illegible]
[illegible]
20 Lord's day [illegible]

Introduction

'Sir, when a man is tired of London, he is tired of life, for there is in London all that life can afford.' Dr Johnson's famous judgement might equally be applied to Samuel Pepys. The range of his interests, the diversity of his pleasures, the vigour of his activity in public and private business, the reflectiveness that led him to record and to evaluate this multiplicity of experience, the communicableness of his humanity, give him a widespread appeal comparable with Shakespeare's. In a sense, Pepys's circle was nothing less than the world of his time. Nothing bored him. Nothing escaped him. Yet for all this universality, he was intensely, supremely, individual. We should know him at once if he came into the room. The portraits of him on pages 5, 12, 100 and 14, one in the prime of life, the others in successful middle age, would in any case make identification easy.

He was born in 1633, the son of a tailor in a very moderate way of business, in Salisbury Court, just off Fleet Street. His mother was of even humbler origin: her relations were butchers, fishmongers and such. The Pepyses extended their connections over a far wider social spectrum. Some of them were tradesmen, like the diarist's father, but a lot of them were lawyers and some were even on the fringes of the landed gentry in East Anglia, where the family is first recorded. However, it was the fortunate marriage of Samuel's great-aunt Paulina into the rich and prominent Montagu family that dealt Pepys his card of entry into the great world of public affairs, where he was to make his name and fortune.

Edward Montagu, Paulina's son, was to be by far the most important member of Pepys's family, but he can hardly be said to belong to Pepys's family circle. Rather, his place is in the circle

James II Receiving the Mathematical Scholars of Christ's Hospital
(detail, see pages 114–15)
Studio of Antonio Verrio, c.1682–8
This bodycolour copy of the original oil painting, which was installed at Christ's Hospital, Horsham, in 1902, was once owned by Pepys. Pepys can be seen holding a scroll in his right hand.

of Pepys's naval and political colleagues. The family circle, Pepys's father and mother, his unsatisfactory brother Tom, and his hardly less unsatisfactory sister Paulina (generally abbreviated to Pall) have left no visual record. Neither have the friends and relations with whom the rising young official enjoyed convivial evenings of music and dancing. Only the bust of his young wife Elizabeth (1640–69) in St Olave's, Hart Street, commissioned by her bereaved husband, survives to remind us of the domesticity brought to life in the *Diary*.

The *Diary* is virtually our only source for Elizabeth Pepys. We see her through the kaleidoscope of her husband's rapidly changing moods, tender and bullying, affectionate and irritable, jealous of her attractiveness to other men and guilty at his own infidelities. Pepys's heroic candour exposes his own meanness, compared with her generosity and readiness to please him. He was very much the senior partner – she was only fifteen when he married her and he was in his early twenties. Her family were impoverished Huguenot refugees, though Elizabeth had had what little education she had managed to acquire at a convent in Paris – another dangerous disrecommendation in the fanatically anti-Catholic England of the seventeenth century. The imprudence of the marriage is evidence of its passion, reinforced by the stormy passages so vividly recorded in the *Diary*. Although Elizabeth was not so much a member of his circle as an equal in it, Pepys did encourage her to share his musical and artistic tastes and admired the promise she showed in singing and painting. Her early death, only a few months after the *Diary* closes in 1669, ended his most intimate relationship.

Of Pepys's boyhood we have virtually no record. A boy of nine when the Civil War broke out in 1642, it seems probable that he was sent to the grammar school in Huntingdon, where his uncle had property nearby. At the end of the war he went to St Paul's and we know that he was still at school there when he witnessed the execution of Charles I in January 1649. Equipped with a leaving exhibition he went up to Magdalene College, Cambridge, taking his degree in 1654. In that year or the next he became some kind of a servant, not a secretary exactly nor yet a steward but something of that order, to Edward Montagu, the Earl of Sandwich and his eminent cousin, eking out this modest position by taking service as a clerk to George Downing (after whom Downing Street is named), then an official in the Exchequer.

When Montagu was charged with taking the fleet over to Holland to bring back Charles II in the spring of 1660, he offered Pepys the post of secretary. From then on Pepys's career was made. Clerk of the Acts, Secretary to the Admiralty, Treasurer of the Tangier Committee, Surveyor-General of the Victualling of the Royal Navy, Clerk of the Privy Seal, the Government jobs came in pell-mell. And each one offered, besides a salary, an almost unlimited opportunity for feathering one's nest. For the rest of his life Pepys was to be comfortably off and latterly very rich.

This enabled him to indulge his pleasures and to cultivate his tastes, even to become a patron: 'a very great cherisher of learned men of whom he had the conversation' as his friend for forty years, John Evelyn, wrote of him on his death in 1703. His superb library, preserved in its entirety at Magdalene College, Cambridge, shows the depth and breadth of his intellectual and literary interests. The *Diary* is eloquent of his passion for the theatre and, above all, for music, 'the thing of the world that I love most'. His eye for painting was keen and he knew most

Samuel Pepys

Unknown artist, c.1665?

Once thought to be the portrait by 'Savill', this portrait was in fact painted at a later date, but nothing is known about its artist or the commission.

of the leading artists of his day. The division between the sciences and the arts, 'the two cultures' in C.P. Snow's famous phrase, had not yet appeared. Pepys was an early Fellow, and ultimately President, of the new-born Royal Society. At the height of the Dutch War, he, the right hand of the Navy as George Monck called him, took the day off to be rowed upriver while reading a treatise on the hydrostatics. His professional life, too, nourished his intellectual curiosity. Not only ships and shipbuilding but the wider implications of sea power led him to amass materials for a 'History of the Marine', which would have taken in, besides ordinary naval history, exploration and discovery, colonisation and seaborne trade.

The *Diary*, to which allusion has already been made, is one of the great texts of English literature, of English history, almost one might say of English civilisation. It is certainly the reason why we have all heard of Pepys. Since it was first published, a century and a half after it had been written, it has never been out of print.

It covers a mere nine years – from January 1660 to May 1669. But what years! The death-throes of the English Republic, the Restoration of the Monarchy in May 1660, the Plague of 1665, the Fire of London in 1666, the great battles of the Second Dutch War, as hard-fought as any in the history of the Royal Navy, the humiliation with which it ended when the Dutch broke into the main fleet base in the Medway and towed away the flagship (her stern can still be seen at the Rijksmuseum in Amsterdam). Through all this period Pepys was uniquely well-placed to observe, and he was one of the most observant men who ever lived. The freedom with which he expressed his opinions of great persons from the King downwards made this

Samuel Pepys
Sir Godfrey Kneller, 1689
Pepys had Kneller paint this portrait and another of his good friend William Hewer, while the two were living together in Clapham.

a highly dangerous document. He always kept it under lock and key and it was written in shorthand, which accounts for its lying unread in his library for more than a century after his death.

Pepys discontinued the *Diary* because eye-trouble convinced him that he was going blind. In fact this cleared up with the help of spectacles. He was to live for another thirty-four years and to become one of the most creative public servants in our history.

Politics and economics – a word only recently coined and hardly in circulation even among educated men – were his constant preoccupation and led him to a range of important friendships and acquaintances. And then there were his day-to-day colleagues at the Navy Board, some of them highly efficient like Sir William Coventry or Sir George Carteret, some of them amiable muddlers like Sir John Mennes. Most important of all there were the Sea Officers as Pepys and his contemporaries called them, Naval officers as we should say: Montagu himself, Monck, Prince Rupert, the Duke of York, Sir Robert Holmes, Sir Christopher Myngs, Sir John Harman, Sir John Narborough and many others. It was an age rich in achievements in every sphere, and in many of them Pepys was either personally engaged or an alert and informed spectator.

BIOGRAPHIES

Edward Montagu, 1st Earl of Sandwich
Sir Peter Lely, *c.*1655–9

NAVAL COLLEAGUES: ADMINISTRATORS, TARPAULINS AND GENTLEMEN

Edward Montagu, 1st Earl of Sandwich (1625–72)

Edward Montagu was one of the star performers in the age of civil war and rapid political change that followed the virtual collapse of Charles I's government in 1641. Raising a regiment for Parliament as a young man of nineteen, he so much impressed Cromwell that he was given a colonelcy in the New Model Army. Under the Protectorate he was made a member of the Council of State, and in 1656 joined with the great admiral Blake in command of the fleet. Robert Blake (1598–1657) was far the greatest admiral that England had yet produced. Alike for his success as a fighting leader, for his grasp of maritime strategy and for the devotion he inspired in his seamen, he is the only possible rival to Nelson. Nelson indeed, never given to false modesty, famously recognised this: 'I do not count myself equal to Blake.' That Blake is so little known to the generality of his countrymen is explained by the fact of his service having been exclusive to the Republic that had been formed on the execution of Charles I. Even as late as 1912, King George V refused to allow a Dreadnought battleship to be named after him.

In 1659, after the death of Oliver and the fall of Richard Cromwell, Montagu commanded the fleet and Monck the army that brought about the immensely popular restoration of Charles II. Monck was made a duke, Montagu an earl, and both were in a position to promote their own friends and relations. It was thus that in 1660 Pepys became Clerk of the Acts, in effect Secretary, to the Navy Board. This is what he meant when he remarked a few years later 'Chance, not merit, brought me into the navy.'

Montagu's absences at sea had opened his eyes to his young cousin's talents as a political observer and reporter. A Commander-in-Chief abroad needed to know what were the pressures on the Government at home and what it was thinking of doing next. Pepys's curiosity, his love of gossip, his eager sociability, combined to make him a marvellous source, as every reader of the *Diary* can see.

Montagu's claims to the supreme command in the Second Dutch War (1665–7) were strong, but room had to be found for the King's brother, James, Duke of York, as Lord High Admiral and for his cousin Prince Rupert. Even so, Montagu distinguished himself in the opening action, the battle off Lowestoft, and was subsequently entrusted with the command of the squadron detailed to intercept De Ruyter, convoying homeward-bound merchantmen from the Dutch East Indies. De Ruyter slipped through, but some rich prizes were taken. Montagu's carelessness in not enforcing the strict regulations to prevent looting was seized on by his enemies. To protect him, Charles II and Clarendon appointed him ambassador to Madrid, where he was a conspicuous success.

Pepys's failure to keep in touch with him during these years of absence led to a coolness between them. On the

Edward Montagu, 1st Earl of Sandwich
after Sir Peter Lely, *c.*1660

outbreak of the Third Dutch War in 1672, Montagu was once again appointed a flag officer under the Duke of York and once again was in the hottest of the initial action off the Suffolk coast, in which he lost his life. He was given a state funeral in Westminster Abbey, a fitting recognition of his outstanding services.

PEPYS ON EDWARD MONTAGU

The *Diary*, Vol. 1, 20 October 1660

To my Lord's by land, calling at several places about business. Where I dined with my Lord and Lady; where he was very merry and did talk very high how he would have a French Cooke and a Master of his Horse, and his lady and child to wear black paches; which methought was strange, but he is become a perfect Courtier; and among other things, my Lady saying that she would have a good Merchant for her daughter Jem, he answered that he would rather see her with a pedlar's pack at her back, so she married a Gentleman rather then that she should marry a Citizen.

Sir William Coventry (1627–86)

Professionalism was the first principle of Pepys's life. More than any other figure in our history he was responsible for professionalising the Royal Navy, that is, making it into a wholetime, permanent force with a career structure. Even in the arts – painting, the theatre, music – in which he was necessarily a dilettante, he expected professionalism in the practitioners whom he admired or patronised. His own career was founded by professionalism. Chance, not merit, may have brought him into the Navy but from the moment he arrived at the Navy Office in Seething Lane, hard by the Tower, he made administrative efficiency and the acquiring of professional knowledge in every department of the Board's responsibilities his first and transcendent objectives.

In this context, Sir William Coventry was the colleague whom Pepys most admired. To a great extent Pepys tried to model himself on him but could not achieve Coventry's high-minded determination not to accept bribes, a principle that Coventry even tried to introduce into government service in exchange for an increase in salaries. Pepys, with his instinct for efficiency, saw the merit of this proposal but was not surprised that it did not find favour. Charles II was hardly a man to clean up the business of government. Coventry, indeed, was a bolder man than his young admirer, as his circumstances enabled him to be. The son of a much respected Lord Keeper under Charles I, his social and financial position left him free to be his own man. As a very young man he had fought for the King and followed Charles II into exile, but, finding no opening for his talents, returned to live quietly under Cromwell. At the Restoration,

Sir William Coventry
John Riley, *c.*1680

James, Duke of York, made him his private secretary as well as his secretary in his capacity as Lord High Admiral. This brought him a place, though not an office, on the Navy Board.

Coventry had been elected to Parliament in 1661, the so-called Long Parliament of the Restoration (it was not dissolved until 1679) where he rapidly made a name as one of the best, perhaps *the* best, debaters. His fearless integrity did not endear him to the King or to the Duke of York, who liked their politicians pliant. On the other hand, his outstanding ability (admitted even by Clarendon, the King's chief minister, who had always disliked him) and his standing in the House of Commons made him a valuable servant. The split came in 1667, when Coventry led the Parliamentary attack on Clarendon, whom everyone (except the Duke of York, who had married his daughter) was glad to make the scapegoat for the misconduct of the Dutch War, culminating in the shame of the Medway disaster. James dismissed his secretary for what he regarded as personal disloyalty, and the King, who had always resented Coventry's dispassionate intelligence, seized the first opportunity of getting rid of him altogether. There was no public servant whom Pepys held in such unqualified esteem: 'the ability and integrity of Sir William Coventry in all the King's concernments I do and must admire.' Coventry himself showed his usual penetration when he told Pepys, at the very moment of his apparent success in the dismissal of Clarendon, 'that the serving a Prince that minds not his business is most unhappy for them that serve him well, and an unhappiness so great that he will never have more to do with a war, under him.'

PEPYS ON WILLIAM COVENTRY
The *Diary*, Vol. 3, 14 September 1662

Thence to St. James's to Mr. Coventry and there stayed talking privately with him an hour in his chamber of the business of our office, and find him to admiration good and industrious, and I think my most true friend in all things that are fair. He tells me freely his mind of every man and in everything.

Sir John Harman (1625–72)

The sea officers with whom Pepys's life was bound up were at the time, and have been generally since, classified under two categories: the Tarpaulins and the Gentlemen. The tarpaulins, as their nickname suggests, were what Pepys called 'bred seamen', that is they had followed the sea as a means of livelihood, in merchant ships or on whaling voyages or less ambitious fishery. Under the aggressive, expansionist foreign policy of Cromwell, the State Navy had grown to a formidable size, offering more or less continuous employment with attractive prospects of wealth and public honour. Most, indeed practically all, the tarpaulins were thus by definition men who had served under the Commonwealth and Protectorate governments, of whom a good example is Sir John Harman. Harman first appears as Captain of a forty-gun ship in the First Dutch War (1652–4), subsequently serving under Blake in the Mediterranean and at the great victory of Santa Cruz in the Canaries, when the entire Spanish plate fleet was sunk while riding at anchor. In the Second and Third Dutch Wars (1665–7 and 1672–4) he was in the thick of the bloodiest actions: in both he was severely wounded and in both he distinguished himself as a flag officer, winning a brilliant victory in the West Indies.

Sir John Harman
Studio of Sir Peter Lely, c.1666

Sir John Mennes
after Sir Anthony van Dyck, c.1640

Sir John Mennes (1599–1671) and William, 2nd Viscount Brouncker (1620–84)

Pepys's professionalism and administrative zeal frequently brought him into collision with his colleagues; older, much more experienced men, such as Sir William Penn and Sir William Batten, both of whom had held high command at sea in the Civil War on the Parliament side, and Sir John Mennes, a Royalist whose career as a sea officer reached back to the reign of James I. Pepys enjoyed his company over a convivial glass: Mennes was an amusing conversationalist and a ready composer of ribald verse, but as an administrator it is impossible to better Sir William Coventry's inspired image: 'like a lapwing; that all he did was to keep a flutter to keep others from the nest that they would find.'

Penn and Batten were tarpaulins of the tarpaulins. They had followed the sea from boyhood, and their familiarity with every detail of seamanship and ship construction meant that Pepys had to address himself to mastering all these technicalities if he was to be able to hold his own at the Navy Board. Mennes was a gentleman officer *par excellence*. It is appropriate that he was the officer entrusted by Charles I with bringing Rubens over to England.

Of his other colleagues in naval administration, one of the most prominent was William, Viscount Brouncker, the first President of the Royal Society. Like Pepys he had an antecedent experience of naval affairs, but a peer who was distinguished in the circle of experimental philosophers might be expected to have something to contribute to the deliberations of the Navy Board. Besides their common interest in science, Brouncker shared Pepys's love and knowledge of music. The curious mixture of insouciant irresponsibility with the formidable skills of Charles II's navy is exemplified by Brouncker's younger brother Henry, a courtier in the suite of the Duke of York. After the great victory off Lowestoft in 1665 when the Dutch, in disorderly flight, were at the mercy of the English, Henry Brouncker, pretending to have the Duke's authority, ordered sail to be shortened, thus allowing the enemy to escape.

OPPOSITE
Frontispiece to 'The History of the Royal-Society of London' by Thomas Sprat (William Brouncker, 2nd Viscount Brouncker; King Charles II; Francis Bacon, 1st Viscount St Alban)
Wenceslaus Hollar after John Evelyn, 1667

ABOVE
William, 2nd Viscount Brouncker
Possibly after Sir Peter Lely, *c.*1674

Sir Robert Holmes (1622–92) and Sir Frescheville Holles (1642–72)

Two gentlemen officers with whom Pepys had somewhat stormy relations were Sir Robert Holmes and Sir Frescheville Holles, arrestingly portrayed in one of Lely's finest double-portraits. A gentleman officer was equally by definition Royalist, not Cromwellian, still less parliamentarian, in political sympathy. Some of them, like Frescheville Holles, were too young to have served in the Civil War but Holmes, as a junior cavalry officer, had won the good opinion of Prince Rupert and had followed him into exile in 1646. When in 1648 a great part of the Parliamentary fleet mutinied and went over to Holland to put itself under the command of the Prince of Wales, the future Charles II, Rupert was appointed to command the ships that did not return to England and their original obedience. Holmes joined him and served under him in precarious buccaneering voyages without any proper base. First of all to Southern Ireland, then Lisbon, then to the Mediterranean, where Blake caught up with them and destroyed all but a couple of ships, then down the Atlantic coast of Africa, across by the Cape Verde islands to the West Indies and back, at last, to the mouth of the Loire in 1652, it was an apprenticeship to seafaring as arduous as that of most tarpaulins and certainly as adventurous. Holmes was at once employed by the restored Monarchy. Experienced sea officers of such impeccable Royalist antecedents were in short supply. He was sent in command of two expeditions down the Atlantic coast of Africa in 1661 and in 1663 in support of the Royal African Company against the much better-established Dutch. On the second voyage he interpreted his instructions in so aggressive a spirit, capturing Dutch forts and making prize of their vessels, as to make a war more or less inevitable. In the course of it Holmes, as Rear-Admiral of the Red, carried out one of the most successful raids against the merchant shipping on which Dutch power was based. Known as 'Holmes's Bonfire', well over a hundred ships went up in smoke in the anchorage of the Vlie, a natural harbour sheltered by the islands of Vlie and Schelling on the coast of Friesland.

But before that Holmes and Pepys had had words at a meeting of the Navy Board in 1663 that might easily, as Pepys apprehensively recorded in the *Diary*, have led to a duel. To Pepys's relief Holmes relented. They were brought into contact again in the Third Dutch War, and, at the very end of Pepys's career, when William III's invasion fleet was in the Channel, both men were unfaltering in their loyalty to James II. In 1690, Pepys even sought Holmes's help in his unavailing attempts to retain a seat in Parliament.

The last of the sea officers here illustrated is Sir Frescheville Holles, Holmes's partner in the double-portrait. He is painted in half-profile, brandishing his sword, perhaps because he had lost his other arm in the Battle of the Four Days (1–4 June 1666). Holles was a courtier-captain who also held a commission in the Guards and sat in Parliament, where as a partisan of the Duke of Buckingham, he was apt to be a vigorous critic of the Navy Board. He was exactly the sort of officer that Pepys was fondest of inveighing against: undisciplined, hard-drinking,

OVERLEAF
Sir Frescheville Holles and Sir Robert Holmes
Sir Peter Lely, *c*.1672

hard-swearing, in a word unprofessional. But his record as a fighting leader was impressive enough for Holmes to choose to be commemorated with him and to commend his service in the opening battle of the Third Dutch War. Two months later, he was killed at the Battle of Sole Bay (May 1672).

PEPYS ON SIR ROBERT HOLMES
The *Diary*, Vol. 7, 24 June 1666

Speaking of Holmes, *how great a man he is, and that he doth for the present, and hath done all this voyage, kept himself in good order and within bounds* – "But," *says he,* "*a Catt will be a Catt still; and some time or other, out his humour must break again.*"

Peter Pett (1610–70)

Professionalism, it has been remarked, was the key to Pepys's own approval, even perhaps where he thought such obvious virtues as courage and honesty were wanting. Such was the case with the famous shipwright, Peter Pett. He was the son of an equally famous shipbuilder, Phineas Pett, and the Pett clan, whose ramifications would baffle all but the most seasoned genealogist, occupied practically all the important positions in the yards along the Thames and the Medway, and had done so well before Pepys came on the scene. In this picture he stands in front of the great and beautiful ship, the *Sovereign of the Seas*, the pride of Charles I's navy, herself asserting in her name the high claims of the Stuart monarchy. Pepys evidently did not like him, and with the rest of his colleagues on the Navy Board was relieved and delighted to have him made another scapegoat for the Medway disaster of 1667, for which they might more justly have been called to account.

All our miscarriages on Pett *must fall:*
His name alone seems fit to answer all.
Whose counsel first did this mad War beget?
Who all commands sold through the Navy? Pett.
Who all our ships exposed in Chatham's Net?
Who should it be but the Phanatick Pett?
Pett, *the Sea Architect, in making Ships,*
Was the first cause of all these Naval slips:
Had he not built, none of these faults had bin;
If no creation, there had been no Sin.

The wit and force of Marvell's satire have assured him his place in history.

Peter Pett *and the* Sovereign *of the* Seas
Sir Peter Lely, *c.*1645–50

PEPYS ON PETER PETT

The *Diary*, Vol. 5, 27 January 1664

He [Pett] told me many stories of the yard; but I do know him so well and had his character given me this morning by Hempson, as well as my own knowledge of him before, that I shall know how to value anything he says either of friendship or other business.

THE KING, THE COURT AND POLITICS

Charles II (1630–85)

Only five years after the Medway disaster, England was again at war with the Dutch and Pepys was again, in administrative terms, the right hand of the Navy. By this time, Sir William Coventry had become the most formidable critic of the King's pro-French policy of the 1670s, and, while Pepys could not afford to support Coventry's opinions in too public a manner, he complained in his Naval Minutes, those private reflections he jotted down mostly in his retirement, of the King's frivolity and, as it seemed to him, sheer irresponsibility.

However, Pepys was impressed by the King's mastery of naval detail and his intellectual apprehension of what it all amounted to (which is what is signified by the (to us) odd use of the word 'mathematic'). He joined him with his brother James, Duke of York, and Pepys's own patron the Earl of Sandwich in a famous judgement: 'The King, Duke and he [Sandwich] the most mathematick Admirals England ever had.' The King, in fact, never commanded a fleet at sea as the other two did, so that the interpretation given above seems inescapable.

Pepys was not the only man to observe this combination of capacity and disinclination to use it. It is the keynote of the prose portrait *The Character of King Charles II*, drawn by one of his ablest ministers, the Marquess of Halifax. Pepys became one of the

ABOVE
Charles II
Studio of John Michael Wright, *c.*1660–5

OPPOSITE
Charles II
Attributed to Thomas Hawker, *c.*1680

most highly placed, and highly paid, servants of the King, but he was never a courtier, still less an intimate. Their relationship was always easy. The King was a shrewd judge of men and knew Pepys's value. He sometimes showed his appreciation but perhaps the nearest approach to intimacy was when in October 1680 he dictated to him his account of his adventures when he was on the run after the Battle of Worcester in 1651.

The King's love of pleasure evoked conflicting reactions in Pepys. On the one hand Pepys envied the King the embraces of Lady Castlemaine: on the other Pepys disapproved of the neglect of business to which the King's love of pleasure contributed.

King Charles II and Colonel William Carlos (Careless) in the Royal Oak
Isaac Fuller, 1660s
This is one of a set of five paintings the depict episodes in Charles II's escape after the Battle of Worcester.

That the King recognised the value of his most expert servant in the most important, and most expensive, of all departments of state is clear from many instances, culminating in the unprecedented appointment, at the very end of Charles II's reign, to the Secretaryship of the Admiralty. It is this professional relation that gives Pepys's portrayal of Charles II its special quality. The King's laziness, his unreliability, his frivolity, are tellingly stated: but his acuteness, his understanding of naval affairs, his coolness in times of danger, are never underplayed.

PEPYS ON CHARLES II
The *Diary*, Vol. 4, 15 May 1663

... the King doth mind nothing but pleasures and hates the very sight or thoughts of business.

James, Duke of York (later King James II)
Sir Peter Lely, c.1665–70

James II (1633–1701)

With Charles II's brother and successor, James, Duke of York, Pepys had a great deal to do. Straightforward to a fault (dissimulation is, as Halifax pointed out in the character of Charles, 'a Jewel of the Crown'), brave, and loyal to the men who served him, he was in most ways the antithesis of his brother. James had real military talent: as a young man in exile he had won golden opinions and rapid promotion in the French army. As an admiral his coolness in action was universally admired and, for so naturally obstinate a man, he showed a wise readiness to learn from the experts who sailed with him just as he did with his brilliant administrators, Coventry and Pepys. Pepys's own loyalty to him was complete. After the Revolution of 1688 he refused to take the oaths to William and Mary, thus exposing himself to the penalty of double taxation as well as ending his official career.

Few English kings have been so totally devoid of political antennae. In spite of ample warning, the Revolution of 1688 came on James II like a thunderclap. The disloyalty of men he had trusted unmanned him. His reactions, inept and indecisive, made the transition to William and Mary easier than anyone could have hoped. He retired to France, making, with French support, an unsuccessful attempt to recover his throne by raising his Irish Catholic subjects against his usurping son-in-law. The Siege of Londonderry and the Battle of the Boyne have left their mark on Anglo-Irish relations.

OVERLEAF
Anne Hyde, Duchess of York, and James, Duke of York (later King James II)
Sir Peter Lely, 1660s

PEPYS ON THE DUKE OF YORK (LATER JAMES II)
The Diary, Vol. 5, 4 June 1664

the Duke of Yorke ... is more himself, and more of judgment is at hand in him, in the middle of a desperate service then at other times – as appeared in the business of Dunkirke, wherein no man ever did braver things or was in hotter service in the close of that day, being surrounded with enemies ... And though he is a man naturally Martiall to the highest degree, yet a man that never in his life talks one word of himself or service of his own ...

James II
Unknown artist,
late seventeenth century

Prince Rupert (1619–82)

With Holmes's patron, Prince Rupert (Charles I's nephew, son of his sister Elizabeth, the Winter Queen, and Frederick, Elector Palatine), Pepys's relations were never happy. In the *Diary* he is dismissed as empty and arrogant: 'Prince Robert [Rupert] doth nothing but swear and laugh a little, with an oath or two, and that's all he doth.' This is Rupert as a fellow member of the Tangier Committee, whose Treasurership Pepys counted 'one of the best flowers in my garden.' When Rupert was Commander-in-Chief in the Second and Third Dutch Wars there was real antagonism; Pepys accusing Rupert of, or implying his responsibility for, mishandling of scarce naval stores while Rupert roundly attacked Pepys for the failure to maintain essential supplies.

Rupert's versatility has been overshadowed by his well-established reputation as the dashing cavalry commander of the Civil War. Dash and daring were by no means his only military qualities. On two crucial occasions his professional advice, against besieging Gloucester in 1643 and against seeking battle at Naseby in 1645, was overridden with disastrous results. His talents as a seaman have been neglected, as have his scientific experiments in surgery conducted on himself and in the development of the mezzotint. Born and brought up abroad, never really at home in English society or in the court of Charles II, he remains aloof, distinguished, solitary.

Prince Rupert, Count Palatine
Gerrit van Honthorst, *c.*1641–2

Prince Rupert, Count Palatine
Studio of Sir Peter Lely, *c.*1670

George Monck, 1st Duke of Albemarle (1608–70)

In the campaign of 1666 Rupert was Joint Commander-in-Chief with George Monck, 1st Duke of Albemarle. Both men ought to have won Pepys's whole-hearted approval, since both were professionals first and last, and Rupert in addition was accomplished both as a scientist and an artist. Both had spent their lives in the profession of arms by land and sea: both had put themselves to school in foreign armies. Monck, as we have seen, was generous in his recognition of Pepys's services, but the compliment was not returned. Monck is repeatedly described as a 'blockhead', though his courage and patriotism are grudgingly conceded. Part of the reason for this may unquestionably be found in the fierce rivalry between Monck and Pepys's patron, Montagu, the two men who had between them brought about the Restoration and were thereafter often at odds over the division of the spoils.

Monck, born into a Devon family of some standing, as a younger son had had to make his own way in the world. To have been raised from the status of a commoner to that of a duke in one stroke, as he was at the Restoration, was a remarkable achievement. While a prisoner of war in the Tower (he had been captured in 1644 as a Royalist officer); he married his washerwoman, who seems to have added ill nature and bad manners to her other disadvantages.

PEPYS ON GEORGE MONCK

The *Diary*, Vol. 8, 23 October 1667

They did also vote this day thanks to be given to the Prince and Duke of Albemarle for their care and conduct in the last year's war – which is a strange act; but I know not how, that blockhead Albemarle hath strange luck to be beloved, though he be, and every man must know, the heaviest man in the world, but stout and honest to his country.

George Monck, 1st Duke of Albemarle
Studio of Sir Peter Lely, 1665–6

Anthony Ashley Cooper, 1st Earl of Shaftesbury (1621–83)

Of all the politicians with whom Pepys had to do (apart from his cousin and Sir William Coventry, who were his close associates); the ablest and most active was Anthony Ashley Cooper, created Baron Ashley in 1661 and Earl of Shaftesbury in 1672. Pepys came across him directly as a colleague on the Tangier Committee and indirectly as Chancellor of the Exchequer from 1661–72 and Lord Chancellor from 1672–3. Shaftesbury, as he is known to history, had changed sides during the Civil War and early established himself as an opponent to the absolutist tendencies of the restored monarchy, particularly as manifested in the heir presumptive, James, Duke of York. In the late years of the reign Shaftesbury was a founder of the Whig party, determined to exclude James from the succession on the grounds of his Roman Catholicism.

The campaign over the Exclusion Bill reminded the nation of the tension that had preceded the Civil War: 'Forty-one is come again.' It reached its crisis at the Parliament of Oxford in 1681, when Shaftesbury and his allies actually appeared in arms. But the King had laid his plans more skilfully than his father and dissolved the Parliament before Shaftesbury could secure his objective – before, indeed, there was any opportunity for motion or debate. Shaftesbury fled the country and the Whigs were in total disarray until James II's undisguised attempt to force a wildly unpopular policy on the country brought about the Revolution of 1688. As a servant of the monarchy and particularly of James, Pepys found himself on the opposite side to Shaftesbury but he clearly recognised his formidable intelligence.

PEPYS ON ANTHONY ASHLEY COOPER

The Diary, Vol. 5, 10 June 1664

Up, and by water to White-hall and there to a Committee of Tanger. And had occasion to see how my Lord Ashwith deports himself; which is very fine endeed, and it joys my heart to see that there is anybody looks so near into the King's business as I perceive he doth in this business of my Lord Peterborough's accounts.

Anthony Ashley Cooper, 1st Earl of Shaftesbury
after John Greenhill, c.1672–3

Edward Hyde, 1st Earl of Clarendon (1609–74)

The other political Titan, an ageing Titan, whom Pepys found much more congenial was Edward Hyde, 1st Earl of Clarendon.

PEPYS ON EDWARD HYDE
The *Diary*, Vol. 7, 13 October 1666

And indeed, I am mad in love with my Lord Chancellor, for he doth comprehend and speak as well, and with the greatest easiness and authority, that ever I saw in my life. I did never observe how much easier a man doth speak, when he knows all the company to be below him, than in him; for though he spoke endeed excellent well, yet his manner and freedom of doing it, as if he played with and was informing only all the rest of the company, was might pretty.

Edward Hyde, 1st Earl of Clarendon
after Adriaen Hanneman, c.1648–55

This is Clarendon at a meeting of the Tangier Committee in 1666, old, arthritic, gouty, out of touch and out of sympathy with the frivolous, dissolute, indecent company preferred by Charles II. The portrait of him here reproduced shows him in the vigour of his prime, one of the wisest, most cultivated, and most articulate of all English statesmen.

Clarendon's misfortune was that he and his friends who did all they could to prevent the Civil War and, once it had started, to end it by negotiation not by military triumph, were never able to get Charles I to back them. Perhaps – who can guess the ebb and flow of that Protean mind? – left to himself, the King would have made ready to do so. But he never was left to himself and, in the opinion of many who knew him, was too distrustful of his own judgement. In any case when he saw that he was likely to be defeated and might be made prisoner, he was clear and emphatic in choosing Hyde as the counsellor and guide for his heir, a choice that was amply vindicated by the Restoration. Clarendon came into power as an old man who had been out of the country for fourteen years. Pepys, for all his unstinted admiration, saw clearly that in the world of intrigue and day-to-day political management, Clarendon was no match for his enemies and rivals. 'My Lord Chancellor is upon his back, past ever getting up again.' Clarendon's fall in 1667, precipitated by the Medway disaster for which, like Pett, he was a convenient scapegoat, opened the way for him in a second efflorescence to produce a literary masterpiece, *The History of the Rebellion and Civil Wars in England*, worthy of the circle of his young manhood, the circle of Selden and Ben Jonson, of Falkland and Chillingworth. The first volume, published a generation after his death, came out in time for Pepys to read it and to write an ecstatic letter of praise to Clarendon's son.

Barbara Palmer, Countess of Castlemaine and Duchess of Cleveland (1640–1709)

Pepys ogled, admired and lusted after women from all walks of life, but he had a special admiration for Barbara Villiers, Countess of Castlemaine and later Duchess of Cleveland. The daughter of the 2nd Viscount Grandison, a Royalist colonel, her beauty was legendary and her life was perhaps the ultimate manifestation of the sexual freedom – or as others saw it, licentiousness – available to some women in the privileged, liberal context of Charles II's court. Mistress to the 2nd Earl of Chesterfield in her teens, she married Roger Palmer, later Earl of Castlemaine, in 1659. She met Charles II shortly after this, and soon became his mistress: the first publicly acknowledged mistress of a king of England for centuries. The first of their five children was born in February 1661. Much to the chagrin of the childless Queen, Barbara was installed as one of her Ladies of the Bedchamber and had a very prominent role in court life throughout the 1660s, until her place in the King's affections was supplanted by others. She was created Duchess of Cleveland in her own right in 1672, provided with numerous pensions, and her children were ennobled and well-married.

Pepys recorded admiring Lady Castlemaine at Whitehall Palace, at the theatre and in the public parks. On one memorable occasion he described seeing her underclothes drying in the sun

Barbara Palmer, Duchess of Cleveland, with her son, Charles Fitzroy, as the Madonna and Child
Sir Peter Lely, c.1664

in the Privy Garden at Whitehall. Ever interested in political as well as personal intrigues, Pepys also noted her involvement in various aspects of court politics. Her political activity seems to have been largely motivated by her desire to secure her own future and that of her children. In practice this meant encouraging particular factions and, perhaps more significantly, providing a means of access to the King. She was notoriously blamed for the downfall of the Earl of Clarendon, Charles II's powerful Lord Chancellor, and while her role has probably been exaggerated, she certainly played a part in facilitating the meetings of his enemies. She also exercised considerable influence in the promotion and demotion of other political figures at various times.

After the end of her relationship with the King in the late 1660s, Barbara's life became, if anything, more colourful. She took numerous lovers, including, apparently, a famous rope-dancer called Jacob Hall, and John Churchill, later Duke of Marlborough (said to be the father to her sixth child, Barbara). A convert to Catholicism, she spent a period of time in France having her daughters educated at a convent and getting involved in more political and sexual intrigue. Back in England in the 1680s she had more affairs and married a bigamist who also started a relationship with her granddaughter. She died of dropsy having nearly reached the age of sixty.

Described by one female acquaintance as 'querilous, fierce, loquacious, excessively fond, or infamously rude ...

Barbara Palmer, Duchess of Cleveland as St Catherine
after Peter Lely, *c.*1666

The extreames of prodigality and covetousness; of love and hatred; of dotage and aversion ... joyn'd together', Barbara Villiers symbolised, both to her contemporaries and to posterity, many of the distinctive qualities of Restoration Britain. Muse to the most successful painter of the day, Peter Lely, she was also the subject of biting and obscene satire, of poetry by Rochester and others, and of censorious writing by the historians Bishop Burnet and Lord Clarendon. But it is Pepys who perhaps sums up most succinctly the ambiguous place she held in the popular imagination: 'But strange it is, how for her beauty I am willing to conster all this to the best and to pity her wherein it is to her hurt, though I know well enough she is a whore.'

Barbara Palmer, Duchess of Cleveland
John Michael Wright, c.1670

Ἡ δὲ μετάνοια αὐτὴ φιλο-
σοφίας ἀρχὴ γίνεται.

SOCIAL LIFE AND INTELLECTUAL PLEASURES

John Evelyn (1620–1706)

John Evelyn was one of the two men (Sir William Coventry is the other) on whom Pepys consciously tried to model himself. In the group portrait, illustrated on page 69, Evelyn, in late middle age, is holding a copy of his famous book on trees, *Silva*. The book symbolises two important sides of Evelyn's nature, the connoisseur *par excellence*, the *arbiter elegantiae* – how inevitable the terms of fashionable European taste – in gardening, sculpture, engraving, and, on the other side, the scientific dendrologist who saw the necessity of a policy for tree planting to the maintenance of a navy composed of wooden ships.

From the first, Pepys and Evelyn were brought together by this consonance of intellectual and aesthetic interests and the conduct of naval affairs. Evelyn had married into a naval family. He had a fine house at Deptford near the navy yard – rented by Peter the Great on his visit to England with his entourage, succinctly described by Evelyn's steward as 'a houseful of Russians, and right nasty'. In the Dutch Wars he served as Commissioner for the Sick and Hurt, and Pepys would have liked to have had him as a colleague on the Navy Board.

....

OPPOSITE
John Evelyn
Robert Walker, 1648

Both men were early and prominent Fellows of the Royal Society and Evelyn's range was, as Pepys would have been the first to admit, far wider and more searching than his own. He was among the earliest champions of the extraordinary gifts of Sir Christopher Wren and the discoverer of Grinling Gibbons. His collection of prints was the model and inspiration for Pepys's.

Pious, refined, delicate – almost, looking at the portrait of him as a young man, one might have said exquisite – he did not share Pepys's avid sexual appetite nor, it must be admitted, his vivacity. Evelyn's *Diary* reads more like a work of reference than record of a stream of consciousness. Some parts of it describing his European travels are indeed copied straight from guidebooks. But when he does sketch a character, for instance Charles II or Arlington, he is not stiff or priggish. The friendship, the real, deep, affectionate friendship, of the two men is one of the great charms of Pepys's circle.

PEPYS ON JOHN EVELYN
The *Diary*, Vol. 6, 5 November 1665

... made a visit to Mr. Evelings, who, among other things, showed me most excellent painting in little – in distemper, Indian Incke – water colours – graveing; and above all, the whole secret of Mezzo Tinto and the manner of it, which is very pretty, and good things done with it. He read to me very much also of his discourse he hath been many years and now is about, about Guardenage; which will be a most noble and pleasant piece. He read me part of a play or two

of his making, very good, but not as he conceits them, I think, to be. He showed me his Hortus hyemalis; *leaves laid up in a book of several plants, kept dry, which preserve Colour however, and look very finely, better than any herball. In fine, a most excellent person he is, and must be allowed a little for a little conceitedness; but he may well be so, being a man so much above others. He read me, though with too much gusto, some little poems of his own, that were not transcendent, yet one or two very pretty Epigrams: among others, of a lady looking in at a grate and being pecked at by an Eagle that was there.*

William Hewer (1642–1715), Sir James Houblon (c.1629–1700), Sir Anthony Deane (c.1638–1721) and Thomas Gale (c.1635–1702)

The group portrait illustrated here represents the circle of Pepys's old age and retirement, yet it preserves the range and diversity of his taste and curiosity and reaches back in some of its members to the days of his early active life at the Navy Board. The portrait of Evelyn, at the top, is surpassed in human warmth only by that of Pepys's loyalist and ablest assistant, Will Hewer, portrayed here in the bottom right-hand corner. Hewer originally joined Pepys as a part-servant, part-office clerk, but rapidly rose to assist and eventually to succeed Pepys in some of his appointments. His uncle had been a leading naval official under the Protectorate, moving at the Restoration to the even more lucrative East India Company. It was from this source that Hewer drew his enormous wealth, enabling him to buy houses to the south of the Strand and a mansion out at Clapham in which Pepys spent his declining years. When the Revolution of 1688 spelled the end of Pepys's career, Hewer wrote him a letter that his old master endorsed 'a letter of great tendernesse at a time of difficulty':

OPPOSITE

Samuel Pepys (centre), with (clockwise) John Evelyn, Sir James Houblon, Will Hewer, Thomas Gale and Sir Anthony Deane

Page from Pepys's print collection ('Portraits, Gentlemen')

a.

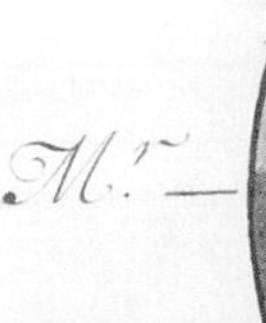

Mr — Evelyn.

Sr Anth. Deane.

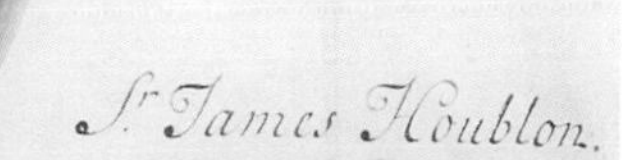

Sr James Houblon.

b.

c.

d.

Mr Pepys.

e.

Dr Gale – Dean of York.

f.

Mr Hewer.

I know you will chearefully acquiesce in what ever circumstance God-Almighty shall think most proper for you, which I hope may prove more to your satisfaction than you can imagine; you may rest assured that I am wholly yours, and that you shall never want the utmost of my constant, faithfull and personall service.

The same loyalty had been shown at an earlier crisis by Sir James Houblon, who is here portrayed immediately above Hewer. The Houblons were a Huguenot émigré family with an astonishing breadth of trading connections and a financial expertise that provided the foundations for the Bank of England. Sir James, one of Pepys's most trusted friends, had risked unpopularity by visiting him in the Tower at the height of the Popish Plot, a ruthless and formidable attempt to frame prominent supporters of the Duke of York as engaged in a treasonable conspiracy. As its name suggests, it was designed to appeal to the fear and hatred of aggressive, militant Catholicism that seemed to seventeenth-century Englishmen to be carrying all before it everywhere in Europe. The cultivated mercantile Huguenot society, at home in European, not merely English, ways of life and thought, was highly congenial to Pepys.

Of the remaining two intimates on this most intimate page, Sir Anthony Deane and Dr Thomas Gale, Deane had shared the dangers of the Popish Plot. Indeed, he had shared almost the whole of Pepys's professional and political career – both had sat in Parliament for the Admiralty borough of Harwich under Charles II and James II. Dean was, above all, an outstanding professional. Among the distinguished English shipwrights of the late seventeenth century Deane stood out, not only for the success of his designs and for the demand he was in (Louis XIV was among his clients) but also for the artistic elegance of his drawings, some of which Pepys collected for his library. Deane was already employed at Woolwich when Pepys was appointed Clerk of the Acts, and they remained colleagues for thirty years and friends for life. But it was very much a professional friendship. Although Deane was elected Fellow of the Royal Society and served on its Council; he does not appear to have had the discursive curiosity so characteristic of its early members.

Thomas Gale was, on the other hand, a more typical Fellow in the variety of his learning. A scholar of Westminster under Dr Busby (who was as famous for flogging his unfortunate pupils as Dr Keate at Eton a century later), he became Regius Professor of Greek at Cambridge and High Master of St Paul's before ending his days as Dean of York. Besides his productive and wide-ranging classical scholarship he was also, like Humphrey Wanley, a notable collector of manuscripts and corresponded with Pepys, whose cousin he had married, in this common interest. His son Roger was as good an antiquary as his father and was one of the young scholars in whom the ageing Pepys took a benevolent interest.

Humphrey Wanley (1672–1726) and Richard Bentley (1662–1742)

Sir Frescheville Holles, the gentleman officer portrayed by Lely (page 34) was the son of a very different sort of man, the antiquary Gervase Holles, whose great collection of manuscript material towards a 'History of Lincolnshire' had been largely destroyed when his house was plundered by Parliamentary troops during the Civil War. Pepys had a number of friends who, like the elder Holles, were active in searching out and preserving manuscripts of historical or literary importance. Among the learned men Pepys cherished, in John Evelyn's phrase, were two of the greatest in our history, Humphrey Wanley, the palaeographer to whose labours the Bodleian and the British Library owe so many of their treasures, and Richard Bentley, the classical scholar who was, after Pepys's death, to become a despotic Master of Trinity College, Cambridge. Both, as can be seen from their dates, were young men when Pepys's official career had come to an end and he had leisure and resources to devote to the branches of learning that had always interested him.

OPPOSITE TOP
Humphrey Wanley
Thomas Hill, 1717

OPPOSITE BOTTOM
Richard Bentley
after Sir James Thornhill, 1710

HUMFREDUS WANLEY
COVENTRIENSIS
1717
Richardus Bentleius Æt: 48. 1710

Dr John Wallis (1616–1703)

Cambridge was Pepys's own university (he had even toyed with the suggestion that he should offer himself as a candidate for the Provostship of King's when it fell vacant in 1681), but it was on Oxford that the scholarly interests of his last years centred. The Bodleian was then by far the greatest library in England and it was there that the splendid portrait of Dr Wallis (a copy of which is shown opposite), which Pepys commissioned from Kneller as a present to the University, was to hang for a couple of centuries. Wallis was one of the founders of the Royal Society and a friend of Pepys for forty years. A man of wide reading and cultivation, his distinction as a mathematician was surpassed only by Isaac Newton (1642–1727), whom Pepys knew well enough to correspond respectfully with about the mathematical probabilities of dicing but with whom he was never intimate. Newton's imaginative and intellectual power was of a different order from Pepys's (and of anybody else's, come to that). But Wallis, who was Savilian Professor of Geometry at Oxford from 1649 to 1703 – an extraordinary tenure – was very much a man of Pepys's world.

Wallis's career was founded on his abilities as a cryptographer. He acted as a kind of one-man Bletchley Park, first for the Parliament in the Civil War, then for Oliver Cromwell, and finally for the restored monarchy. Indeed, his services were, after 1688, put at the disposal of William III. To survive as a trusted servant of so many and such different regimes called for tact and judgement as well as professional skill. Wallis always refused to divulge his methods and, a naturally humane man, could always leave passages undecoded if they were likely to cause avoidable trouble.

Dr John Wallis
after Sir Godfrey Kneller, 1701

Sir William Petty (1623–87)

Another member of this remarkable group of brilliant and original minds with whom Pepys was on the friendliest terms was Sir William Petty. Petty, like Wallis, was largely self-educated but, like him, was appointed to a Professorship at Oxford (that of Anatomy), in 1651. Although he too was of a strongly mathematical turn of mind, applying or attempting to apply mathematics to such diverse subjects as social statistics, economics and even sense data such as taste or smell, he combined this speculative intelligence with a strongly practical and observant curiosity. The two sides of his nature were profitably engaged when, after serving as physician to Cromwell's army in Ireland, he was commissioned to make a survey of the conquered country, in order to divide the estates of the losers between the army and others who claimed a share in the loot. The speed and accuracy with which he did this won universal admiration, but he did not neglect the opportunity of making a handsome fortune for himself. Back in England at the Restoration, he devoted a good deal of time and ingenuity to the design of a ship with a double-keel. Both Charles II and Pepys were much impressed and several experimental vessels were built, though ultimately without success. Much more productively, Petty joined with his friend Major Graunt in the first serious attempt at a scientific and mathematical study of social statistics, *Some Observations on the Bills of Mortality*. 'Political Arithmetic' as Petty called it had taken root.

Everybody – Charles II, Pepys, Evelyn, John Aubrey – agreed that Petty was marvellous company. 'He can be excellent Droll (if he haz a mind to it) and will preach *extempore* incomparably, either the Presbyterian way, Independent, Cappucin frier or Jesuite.'

No doubt it was only his earlier death that prevented his portrait appearing in the knot of close friends that Pepys grouped round himself on the page from his print collection (reproduced on page 69).

Sir William Petty
Isaac Fuller, *c.*1640–51

Thomas Ken
F. Scheffer, *c.*1700

Thomas Ken (1637–1711)

The *Diary* tells us a great deal about the common life of the members of the Navy Board, living cheek by jowl in the handsome, well-appointed houses that went with the job. Another perquisite was the Navy Officer pew in the parish church of St Olave's, Hart Street, where the bust of Elizabeth was so placed that her bereaved husband could see it at his weekly devotions. For a man of so pronounced an anti-clerical turn of mind and a far from other-worldly disposition, Pepys was an indefatigable sermon-taster. One of the clergymen whom he respected both as an intellect and as a man was Thomas Ken, whom he got to know very well when they were both sent out in 1683 to assist Lord Dartmouth in the evacuation of the short-lived colony of Tangier.

Ken was a Fellow of Winchester, publishing in 1674 his *Manual of Prayers for Winchester Scholars* to which he subsequently added the famous Morning and Evening hymns, 'Awake, my Soul' and 'Glory to thee, my God, this night,' which are still sung. As a Canon of Winchester he refused the hospitality of his house to the King's mistress, Nell Gwyn, when the Court was paying a visit. Charles II, whose choice of bishops was commended by Dr Johnson, ordered that the next vacancy on the bench should go 'to the little black fellow that refused his lodging to poor Nelly'. Ken had previously dared to reprove William, Prince of Orange, the future William III, for his unkind treatment of his wife. William, though angry, admired his courage and, after 1688, did what he could to induce Ken (who was one of the seven bishops who had stood out against James II's Romanizing policy) to remain in his see. But Ken, like Pepys, felt unable to take the oath, having sworn fealty to James II.

Sir Godfrey Kneller (1646–1723) and Sir Peter Lely (1618–80)

The men whose portraits are to be found in the page from Pepys's own collection (page 69) were all of them either (where they were not both) professional colleagues or men of congruent tastes and interests with whom Pepys was in regular contact. This circle was enriched by tangential figures, such as Lord Somers (1651–1716), the Whig Lord Chancellor who was also President of the Royal Society, a connoisseur and man of learning, but also with much closer contacts, such as that with Sir Godfrey Kneller from whom Pepys commissioned portraits of himself, of John Evelyn, of Dr Wallis and of James II. The King was sitting to the painter for this very picture when he heard that William of Orange had landed at Torbay.

Kneller's productivity was enormous and his temper easy. His greater predecessor as the favourite of Court and of high society, Sir Peter Lely, was, in Pepys's opinion, 'mighty proud and full of state', a judgement that seems consonant with the self-portraits here reproduced. At the same time Pepys had no reservations about his pictures 'without doubt much beyond Mr Hales's' (whom he had commissioned to paint the famous portrait of himself (page 5) and that of his wife, destroyed, it is said, by an infuriated or inebriated cook, in the next century). Pepys also considered Lely far superior – 'Lord, the difference there is between their two works' – to John Michael Wright (1617–94), a portraitist much favoured by Cromwell's family and court as well as by that of Charles II. Pepys particularly admired Lely's portrait of Sandwich, his cousin and patron, 'very well done, and am with child till I get copyed out' – a request that was soon granted: the copy, made by Emmanuel de Critz (1608–65), now hangs at Audley End.

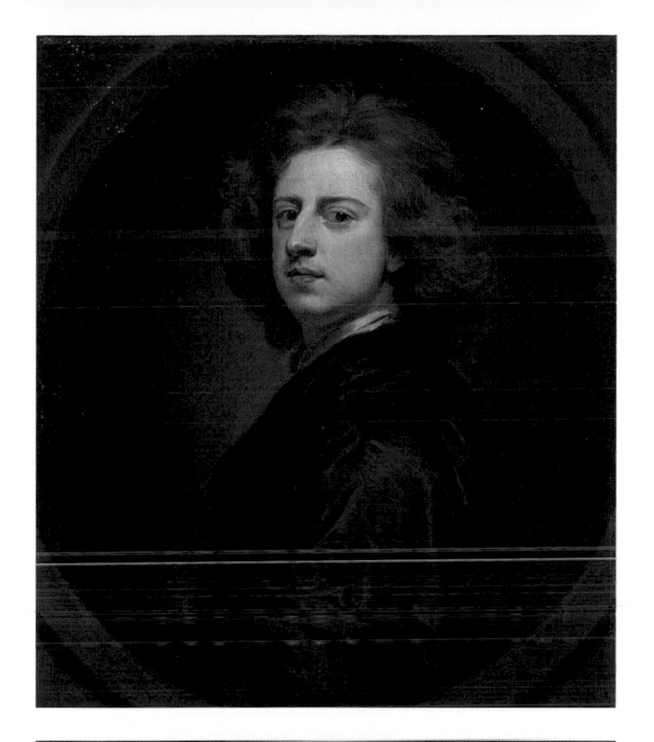

TOP
Sir Godfrey Kneller
Self-portrait, 1685

BOTTOM
Sir Peter Lely
Self-portrait, *c.*1660

Henry Purcell (1659–95)

Music, of all the arts, was easily Pepys's favourite. It permeated his domestic and family life – social evenings were incomplete without instrumental music and even solitude could be enriched by singing (Pepys was a bass who could take that part in the choral services of the Chapel Royal). The greatest musician of his day, Henry Purcell was not, so far as we know, a friend or even an acquaintance of Pepys. But Pepys certainly knew of him, since both Purcell's father and uncle were musicians in the service of the court or the Chapel Royal. Some of his compositions are to be found in the musical collection that Pepys took such trouble to preserve and transcribe for his library – it was another interest that he shared with his cousin, Sandwich, whose own journal as ambassador of Madrid is full of details and drawings of Spanish musical instruments as well as of accounts of his own enjoyment of playing the guitar. 'Musick,' wrote Pepys reflectively in his old age, 'a science peculiarly productive of a pleasure that no state of life, publick or private, secular or sacred: no difference of age or season; no temper of man's or condition of health exempt from present anguish; nor lastly, distinction of quality, renders either improper, untimely or unentertaining.'

Henry Purcell
by or after John Closterman, 1695

Thomas Killigrew (1612–83)

When it came to entertainment it was to the theatre that Pepys, especially the young Pepys, eagerly hurried. Besides the dramatic or comic spell it cast on an audience starved of such excitements (the Puritans had closed the theatres for the twenty years that had preceded the Restoration) there was, once again, the pleasure of music and the allure of beautiful actresses. It was from the stage that Charles II had chosen two of his principal mistresses, Moll Davis (c.1651–1708) and Nell Gwyn (1651?–87) – 'pretty, witty Nell' as Pepys called her. He did not himself fly so high in his amours, but some of the ladies who gave Elizabeth Pepys grounds for doubting her husband's fidelity were connected with the stage.

The one most frequently mentioned in the *Diary*, Elizabeth Knepp, was a member of the company put together by Thomas Killigrew, known as the King's Company, the rivals of the only other licensed body, the Duke's Company, run by Sir William Davenant. Killigrew, born into an aristocratic Cornish family, had begun to write plays before the Civil War. As a page to Charles I he was an avowed Royalist and followed Charles II into exile, acting for a time as his representative in Venice. But his disreputable conduct led to his expulsion from the Republic. He continued to write plays, some of them obscene, and enjoyed the King's favour as a witty companion who was allowed all the licence of a court jester. In 1663 he built the Theatre Royal, burned down a few years later, on the site of the present Drury Lane Theatre, in which he delighted Pepys and other theatregoers by the innovation of movable scenery. In his conversations with Pepys, who found him 'a merry droll', he emphasised the importance of music and singing in theatrical presentations (particularly praising the talents of Mrs Knepp) and talked of producing an Italian opera, which seems to have come to nothing. He and his family exemplify the drunken, dissolute side of Restoration society of which Pepys's closest friends, such as Coventry, Evelyn and Houblon, severely disapproved, but which the King himself freely countenanced.

Thomas Killigrew
William Sheppard, 1650

Elizabeth Pepys (1640–69)

The daughter of an aristocratic but impoverished Huguenot father and an English, probably Catholic mother, Elizabeth de St Michel's early years were spent in Devon, Germany, Flanders, Ireland and Paris (where she was briefly put in a convent by her mother), before she was brought to London, along with her brother Balthasar, by their father. It was there that she met Pepys, under unknown circumstances, and married him in a private religious ceremony in October 1655. Given the poverty of her family, and Pepys's own situation (employed by the Earl of Sandwich but living in a single attic room in Whitehall), the marriage must have been prompted by love rather than more practical considerations. However, Elizabeth, who turned fifteen shortly after her marriage, found these early years so difficult that in 1657 she left Pepys for a period of some months, returning to her parents.

Elizabeth was back with Pepys by December of that year, and the move in the following year to a house in Axe Yard, and subsequently to a bigger house in Seething Lane, must have made life easier for her. As Pepys's prosperity grew, he was able to employ more servants, which lifted some of the domestic burden from Elizabeth, although it led to other problems. Pepys seems to have had very few female servants whom he did not try to seduce. Elizabeth suspected and in some cases knew what was going on, and she did not choose to overlook it. Pepys, for his own part, was jealous of Elizabeth, suspecting her dancing master and her drawing master, trying to keep her from going out too much, and worrying about her having attractive clothes. But in spite of their turbulent domestic life, Pepys's *Diary* and letters written by him after her death suggest that there was real affection between the couple and that he did – albeit inconsistently – try to provide for Elizabeth the kind of life and interests that she desired. Pepys records her independent spirit and hot temper, but also her kindness and generosity, as well as her linguistic, musical and artistic abilities. The fact that she had no children must have been a concern for them both, but there is no evidence that Pepys, like some men of that period, blamed her, and when she died at the age of twenty-nine, he was genuinely grief-stricken.

Elizabeth Pepys
after a marble attributed to John Bushnell, 1672
Elizabeth Pepys died at the age of twenty-nine, shortly after Pepys stopped writing his *Diary*. This bust is a cast of the monument Pepys commissioned for her tomb in St Olave's, Hart Street.

Nell Gwyn (1651?–87) and Moll Davis (c.1651–1708)

In the history of British theatre, 1660 was a notable year not just because that was when the public theatres were re-opened after eighteen years of closure. With the opening of the theatres came a remarkable innovation: for the first time, women began to act on stage in public. Women had taken part privately in the elaborate musical, theatrical court entertainments known as 'masques' in the earlier Stuart courts, but in the public theatres female parts were invariably played by men or boys. The more tolerant character of the new regime must have been evident almost immediately, as the theatre companies were employing actresses before the end of 1660. By 1662, actresses had come to seem a necessity, and the King decreed that from thence all female parts were, by law, to be played by women.

Of all the women in that first generation to act, the most famous is Nell Gwyn, although her fame rests more on her legendary social rise from orange-seller to mistress of the King than on her acting skills. Her early life is obscure, although Pepys had heard that she was brought up in a brothel. She had moved from selling oranges outside the King's Theatre to acting in it by about 1664, and Pepys first met her the following year. He thought Nell very skilled at comic roles, although completely unsuited to serious ones and, ironically, he particularly enjoyed seeing her acting boys' parts. By contrast, Mary, or Moll Davis, another young woman of obscure origins, who acted at the rival Duke's Theatre, was admired by Pepys primarily for her fine dancing. The small group of women actors at this time must all have known each other, and Pepys comments on them watching the performances

Nell Gywn

Simon Verelst, c.1680

Nell Gwyn was painted on several occasions by Simon Verelst, a Dutch painter who arrived in England as a specialist flower painter but appears to have soon turned to portraiture.

of their rivals, but what brought Mary and Nell into particular competition was that they both came to the attention of the King and became his mistresses.

There seems to have been an expectation that women who acted on stage would be available to men in other ways as well. Pepys records kissing Nell and watching her get dressed, and he had an affair with her colleague Elizabeth Knipp (d.1681). Charles II summoned first Moll and then Nell to him in 1668–9, when his relationship with Barbara Villiers was waning. Both women bore the King children: Nell, Charles Beauclerk, later 1st Duke of St Albans (1670–1726), and James, Lord Beauclerk (1709–87); and Moll, Lady Mary Tudor, later Countess of Derwentwater (1673–1726). Although Moll's relationship with the King lasted for some years, she did not capture the public imagination, either in her lifetime or subsequently, in the way that Nell Gwyn did. While many of the stories told about Nell may be fictitious, the fact that she attracted such legends says much about her charisma and the skilful way she negotiated her place in the King's affections and his financial largesse. Dubbed by Pepys 'pretty, witty Nell', she had a reputation for honesty, generosity and good humour, and these qualities, as well as her Protestantism, were contrasted in popular satire with those of the reigning mistress of the 1670s, the French Catholic Louise de Kéroualle, Duchess of Portsmouth (1649–1734).

P Lelij Pinxit.
The Sculpters part is done the features hitt
of Ma. am Gwin ; No Arte can shew her Will ,
G Valck Sculp et ex.

Nell Gywn
Gerard Valck after Sir Peter Lely, c.1673

Moll Davis
Published by Richard Tompson after Sir Peter Lely, c.1674

Moll Davis
after Sir Peter Lely, *c.*1665–70

Pepys and the Royal Society

While Pepys could by no means be regarded as a scientist, like many of his contemporaries in Restoration Britain he took a lively interest in what would today be regarded as scientific enquiry. The Royal Society had been established in 1660 to provide a forum for what was termed a 'new philosophy', in which greater understanding of the world was sought through systematic observation and experimentation, based on principles expounded by, in particular, Francis Bacon, Viscount St Alban (1561–1626). At first 'a Colledge for the Promoting of Physico-Mathematicall Experimentall Learning', it gained royal patronage from the King himself in 1662. Pepys, whose naval colleague Viscount Brouncker was the first President, described its members as 'virtuosi' and evidently admired them; he was elected to its fellowship in 1665.

In his Diary, Pepys describes various demonstrations and experiments he witnessed at Royal Society meetings, as well as discussions he had with other fellows. While he often did not really understand the significance of what he was seeing, he found many of the experiments 'mighty pretty', and bought books to try to expand his understanding. In fact some of the activities of the Royal Society were hardly scientific at all; however, besides these genuine but misguided efforts, there were also many really important discoveries. Christopher Wren (1632–1723), Robert Boyle (1627–91), Edmond Halley (1656–1742), Robert Hooke (1635–1703) and Isaac Newton (1642–1727) were all fellows during Pepys's time at the Society. The polymath Robert Hooke was the first of these men to be noted by Pepys, who described him in 1665 as '... Mr Hooke, who is the most,

Sir Isaac Newton
Sir Godfrey Kneller, 1702

and promises the least, of any man in the world that ever I saw' (15 February). Pepys bought and avidly read his *Micrographia*; he also bought a version of the perspective drawing instrument invented by the architect and mathematician Christopher Wren, and later corresponded with him. Robert Boyle's experiments with an air pump were regularly demonstrated at early Society meetings, and Pepys also bought his book, *Experiments and Considerations Touching Colours* (1664), which he described as 'so chymical, that I can understand but little of it, but understand enough to see that he is a most excellent man'.

In 1684 Pepys was elected President, not because of his knowledge or expertise, but probably in recognition of his administrative skills, which he employed very effectively to the benefit of the Society. Under his leadership, the Society agreed to publish (although not to pay for) Newton's *Principia* (1687), one of the most influential mathematical books ever written, and thus Pepys's name appears on its title page. *Principia* was paid for by Newton's friend the astronomer Edmond Halley (1656–1742), at that time a salaried clerk to the Society, but also with an independent income. Pepys retained an interest in the Society's activities to the end of his life, and an admiration for these extraordinary men, their discoveries and inventions, although he was never fully able to appreciate the lasting impact their work would have.

Sir Christopher Wren
Sir Godfrey Kneller, 1711

Afterword

Enough has been said to justify the claim that Pepys's circle was as wide as that of any man of his time. To have corresponded with Newton, to have gossiped and cracked jokes with hangers-on of Charles II's court, to have listened, rapt, to the music of Purcell, Blow and Matthew Locke, to have frequented the studios of Lely and Kneller, to have sat in council with Clarendon and Shaftesbury, to have managed the conduct of naval warfare with Monck and Prince Rupert, to have watched Charles II and James II at close quarters in times of grave crisis that threatened the stability of the throne, to have – but, easy as it would be to extend this catalogue, enough is enough. The range of Pepys's pleasures as of his business, of his intellectual and aesthetic concerns, encompasses his age.

OPPOSITE

Book plate showing Pepys's initials

probably by Robert White, late seventeenth century

This bookplate can be found at the end of most volumes of the *Diary* held at Magdalene College, Cambridge.

Mens cujusque is est Quisque

Samuel Pepys
attributed to John Riley, *c.*1690

Pepys and the Restoration Art World

Catharine MacLeod

Samuel Pepys's *Diary* testifies to an active and critical fascination with the contemporary art world. His lively curiosity about people, and his concern with the development of his and his wife's cultural lives, stimulated a wide-ranging interest in oil paintings, miniatures, drawings, prints and sculpture, as well as in the artists who made these works and the sitters depicted by portraitists. Pepys sat for his own portrait numerous times, and had his wife Elizabeth painted by several different artists. He arranged for Elizabeth to learn to draw, an accomplishment that was becoming increasingly fashionable among prosperous women at the time. In later life, he assembled the most important collection of prints to survive from the seventeenth century. Throughout his life he appears to have enjoyed discussing art and art theory with artists, connoisseurs, collectors and other knowledgeable acquaintances, most notably his friend John Evelyn (1620–1706). For Pepys, knowledge and discernment about art was an essential quality in a cultivated man, but in addition, art in a variety of forms – and the individuals associated with it – clearly gave him enormous pleasure.

In the seventeenth century, artists' studios were run rather like commercial galleries today: they were not only places where commissions could be arranged, but also where works could be bought from stock or simply admired. Painters were also often collectors in their own right, and dealers in paintings and drawings by others. Pepys took advantage of the opportunities thus afforded to visit a number of artists in their studios, often recording his views on their accomplishments and their lifestyles, as well as on their work, in his *Diary*. Among those he visited were the émigré Dutch landscape painter Jan Looten (*c*.1618–*c*.1681), whose works he found he did not admire, and another Dutch émigré, the still-life and portrait painter Simon Verelst (*c*.1644–*c*.1710), a flower painting by whom he felt was 'worth going twenty miles to see'. On the whole, Pepys's judgements of art were in line with the majority of his contemporaries; the art he liked was usually the most fashionable. He visited the house and studio of Sir Peter Lely (1618–80), Principal Painter to the King and the most successful portrait painter of the day, on several occasions, commenting on his fine collection of paintings, his lavishly laid supper table, and his proud demeanour, as well as his portraits. He seems to have thought little of the work of John Michael Wright (1617–94), another successful and accomplished portraitist, by comparison; but Wright's work was stylistically outside the mainstream of court portraiture, and Pepys may have found it just too unusual for his taste.

Pepys was drawn to visit Lely's house in Covent Garden both by his interest in the artist and by the subject matter of his paintings. In 1666 he saw Lely's set of portraits of the so-called Flagmen of Lowestoft (see a copy of one on page 27) in the early stages of production there. Commissioned by Pepys's employer, the Duke of York, these were portraits of thirteen naval officers who had fought at the Battle of Lowestoft in 1665. Pepys's work for the navy as well as knowledge of these men must have made the portraits of particular interest. But it was Lely's paintings of women that really attracted Pepys's attention. He commented on another occasion that a group of portraits of court women by Lely, hung in the Duke and Duchess of York's apartments, were

Barbara Palmer (née Villiers), Duchess of Cleveland
William Faithorne after Sir Peter Lely, 1666

'good, but not like'. However, when he described a portrait in Lely's studio as 'the so much by me desired picture of my Lady Castlemayne', he was clearly conflating his admiration for both painting and sitter. His thoughts about – and indeed feelings for – Barbara Palmer, née Villiers, Lady Castlemaine (1640–1709), the King's principal mistress in the 1660s, are expressed at various points in the *Diary* and led him to pursue his desire for ownership of her portrait in a number of ways. In the end, he lowered his sights from a full-length oil painting by Lely, to a coloured chalk copy of Lely's painting by the engraver William Faithorne (*c*.1620–91), and eventually settled instead for three impressions of Faithorne's print of Castlemaine, one of which he had varnished and framed, to be hung on the wall.

Lely made it clear to Pepys on several occasions how busy he was. This, and probably also the cost of his work, put it out of the reach of Pepys in the 1660s. The first portraits he is known to have commissioned were oil paintings of himself and his wife from a now almost entirely unknown artist called Savill, who charged only £6 for the two portraits, whereas Lely was already charging £10 each for a half-length portrait ten years earlier. The paintings by Savill are now lost, but we know from the *Diary* that Elizabeth's portrait included her little black dog on her lap, and Pepys himself was shown with his lute. Pepys also records, however, that he thought Savill woefully ignorant of certain aspects of art, notably 'skill in shadows', and consequently was very frustrated by the quality of his conversation with the artist

OPPOSITE
Elizabeth Pepys
James Thomson after John Hales, published January 1828

Hailes pinx.t T. Thomson sculp.t

ELIZABETH PEPYS.

From the original in the possession of S. P. Cockerell, Esq.r

Published by Henry Colburn, London, Jan.y 1828.

about this subject; it is clear from this and other references in his *Diary* that Pepys valued artists' all-round accomplishment and ability to converse intelligently about their work almost as much as their abilities with a brush. He gave Savill various tips for improving the portraits, and although he was satisfied enough with the final result to hang the paintings in his dining room and to commission an additional miniature portrait of himself, for which he had more sittings, once he had paid for the miniature he appears not to have had further dealings with Savill.

Pepys had a much more positive and fruitful relationship with the next artist he sat to: John Hales's (1600–79), a well-established painter who had worked throughout the Interregnum period as a portraitist and copyist of Van Dyck. Pepys commissioned from Hales (or Hayls) portraits of himself and Elizabeth. The entries he made in the *Diary* about the progress of the portraits reveal how engaged he was with their development. Elizabeth Pepys was painted in the guise of St Catherine, in imitation of a portrait they had seen of 'Lady Peters'; this was a fashionable portrait type for women at that period, notionally in homage to the Queen, Catherine of Braganza. He described the sittings for his own portrait (pages 5–7) – 'I sit to have it full of shadows, and do almost break my neck looking over my shoulder to make the posture for him to work by' – and later asked Hales to alter the background from a landscape to a plain interior, against the artist's better judgement. In spite of these complaints and interventions, Pepys's affability and perhaps the artist's tolerance ensured that they had developed a friendship by the end of the process; no doubt Pepys kept to himself a judgement that he made on a subsequent visit to Lely's studio: 'endeed, his pictures are without doubt much beyond Mr. Hales's, I think I may say I am convinced'.

Frances Talbot (née Jenyns (Jennings)), Duchess of Tyrconnel (formerly Lady Hamilton)
Samuel Cooper, *c.*1665

Through John Hales, Pepys met the miniature painter Samuel Cooper (1607/8–72), a figure of international reputation. His delight in Hales's portrait of Elizabeth led him to commission her portrait again, this time in miniature by Cooper. This took at least seven sittings, during which Pepys commented repeatedly on Cooper's skill as a painter, but was less convinced by the work as a likeness. However, Cooper's additional cultural skills impressed Pepys very favourably: 'but now I understand his great skill in music, his playing and setting to the French lute most excellently – and speaks French; and endeed is an excellent man.' This was of course at least the second time Pepys had commissioned a miniature, although Savill's small portrait of Pepys was probably just a small-scale work in oils. Miniatures like Cooper's, a distinct type of object painted with enormous refinement in watercolour on vellum, were an important part of portrait production in seventeenth-century Britain, and a genre in which the British were regarded as excelling. They were usually set inside lockets, and worn on the clothing, or kept in drawers or on the walls of small cabinet rooms, to be shown only to a select few, unlike the more publicly visible oil paintings.

Like an increasing number of fashionable and leisured women of the day, Elizabeth Pepys set about learning to 'limn', or to paint miniatures. That it was this particular art form she learned reflects the fact that miniature painting had, at least since the later sixteenth century, slightly more respectable, or more specifically gentlemanly, associations than oil painting. In addition to being seen as an especially refined genre, the equipment and materials used by miniaturists were relatively small and clean, and no special studio space was required. It was thus a particularly suitable occupation for a gentleman

Samuel Pepys ivory medallion
Jean Cavalier, 1688

or gentlewoman amateur. Pepys felt that Elizabeth showed an aptitude for the art, and he was initially proud of her work. In his characteristic way, however, he became jealous of her drawing master, the miniaturist and print-seller Alexander Browne (d.1706). Just as with her dancing teacher Mr Pembleton, on the basis of apparently no evidence at all, he suspected that the time they spent together was not entirely devoted to drawing. They had a number of arguments about whether they should invite Browne to dinner, and in the end the lessons seem to have stopped after about a year.

Another small form of portraiture that was becoming increasingly popular at this time was the medal, and, characteristically, Pepys took an interest in the most fashionable productions in this genre as well. In order to improve the quality of medal-making after his restoration to the throne in 1660, King Charles II had employed a family of Flemish medallists, John (1631–1703), Joseph (1635–1703) and Philip Roettier (1640–1718). John became the most prominent of the three brothers, and his medallic work was much admired by Pepys, who referred to him in 1666 as 'the famous engraver' and his medals, which he went to see at the Royal Mint, as 'some of the finest pieces of work in embossed work that ever I did see in my life, for fineness and smallness of the images thereon'. He had previously admired Roettier's medallic portraits of the King and made an interesting comparison between them and the earlier portrait medals of Oliver Cromwell by Thomas Simon (1618–65), observing that Roettiers' medals of Charles were 'the better, because the sweeter of the two' but that he thought Simon's medals of Cromwell were better likenesses. Pepys later commented on Roettier's 'Peace of Breda' medal, on which was a figure of Britannia, modelled on a court beauty, Frances Stuart (later Duchess of Richmond, 1647–1702): 'at my goldsmith's did observe the King's new Medall, where in little, there is Mrs. Steward's face, as well done as ever I saw anything in my whole life, I think – and a pretty thing it is that he should choose her face to represent Britannia by.'

Pepys's interest in art after he finished writing the *Diary* in 1669 is evidenced mainly by comments in letters and surviving portraits and other works. As he progressed in his career he

OPPOSITE
Samuel Pepys
Robert White after Sir Godfrey Kneller, published 1690

SAM·PEPYS·CAR·ET·IAC·ANGL·REGIB·A·SECRETIS·ADMIRALIÆ
G·Kneller pinx·
R·White sculp·
Mens cujusque is est Quisque

seems to have been able to afford more fashionable artists, having himself been painted by the German émigré Godfrey Kneller (1646–1723, page 14) in 1689, the year in which the artist was made Principal Painter to King William III. Pepys also commissioned portraits of others from Kneller, including his friend John Evelyn, King James II and the mathematician John Wallis. For the portrait of Wallis, a gift to the Bodleian Library, Pepys considered using another popular German émigré artist, John Closterman (1660–1711). More dramatically, Pepys commissioned the Italian painter Antonio Verrio (*c.*1639–1707), known for his huge decorative schemes for royal palaces, to produce a vast group portrait commemorating the foundation of the Royal Mathematical School at Christ's Hospital. Measuring about twenty-six metres long, it includes among the many figures a portrait of Pepys himself (page 9). Pepys had a reduced version made in gouache for himself (pages 114–5). At the other end of the spectrum, his portrait was also carved on a small ivory medallion by Jean Cavalier (1660?–1699) and later, probably posthumously, by David Le Marchand (1674–1726).

Pepys's interest in painting extended beyond portraiture. His *Diary* records his admiration of the allegorical paintings done by Robert Streater (1621–79) for the Sheldonian Theatre in Oxford, and he had landscape paintings made for his dining room by Hendrick Danckerts (*c.*1625–80). In later life he acquired seascapes, but his fascination with people led him back time and again to portraiture, and of the sixty-one paintings he owned at his death, just over half were portraits. Among the volumes in the library Pepys left to Magdalene College, Cambridge, however, is his most lasting legacy to the history of art: the twelve volumes of his print collection, one of the biggest collections of prints assembled in seventeenth-century England, and the most complete to survive. Many of these prints are portraits, although there are also topographical prints, frontispieces and many other subjects. Although Pepys was aware of the potential artistry in printmaking, the way in which his prints were acquired and arranged in the albums suggests that he thought of them primarily as illustrative of various aspects of life and significant individuals, both contemporary to him and in the past, and that the stimulus to forming the collection was as much an impulse for taxonomy and a desire for completeness as an admiration of particular works. However, for subsequent scholars of the art of the seventeenth century, Pepys's collection provides a unique resource for the early decades of printmaking and print collecting in Britain. Along with his *Diary*, the remaining letters and the works of art that he owned, the print collection gives a unique insight into the life of this remarkable man and the extraordinary times in which he lived.

James II Receiving the Mathematical Scholars of Christ's Hospital
Studio of Antonio Verrio, *c.*1682–8 (bodycolour copy)

SUGGESTIONS FOR FURTHER READING

Far the most comprehensive single source of information about every aspect of Pepys's world is the Companion Volume (vol.10, Bell & Hyman, London, 1983) to the great edition of the *Diary* by Robert Latham and William Matthews. It is, however, designed for reference, not for continuous reading.

The text of the *Diary* itself in the preceding nine volumes (1970–76) is, of course, incomparable – and the annotation of the Latham and Matthews' edition delightfully removes every difficulty.

Of biographies, Sir Arthur Bryant's three volumes, *Pepys: The Man in the Making* (1933), *The Years of Peril* (1935) and *The Saviour of the Navy* (1938), published by Cambridge University Press, have, for all their copiousness and colour, the disadvantage of incompleteness. The third volume ends with Pepys's fall from office in 1699. The present writer's *Pepys: A Biography* (Hodder & Stoughton, London 1974, several times reissued under different imprints) contains two chapters directly bearing on the friendships and interests of his long retirement.

Tomalin, Claire, *Samuel Pepys The Unequalled Self* (Viking, Penguin Books, London, 2002)
John Ingamells, *Later Stuart Portraits 1685–1714* (National Portrait Gallery, London, 2010)

For a general survey of the period, David Ogg's *England in the Reign of Charles II* (Clarendon Press, Oxford, 1934; reprinted 1966) offers a panorama appropriate to Pepys's many-sidedness.

LIST OF ILLUSTRATIONS

p.5 Samuel Pepys, John Hales, 1666. Oil on canvas, 756 x 629mm. © National Portrait Gallery, London (NPG 211)

p.7 Diary extract from 17 March 1666, Samuel Pepys. The Pepys Library, Magdalene College, Cambridge

p.9 *James II Receiving the Mathematical Scholars of Christ's Hospital* (detail), studio of Antonio Verrio, *c*.1682–8. Gouache, watercolour and graphite on paper mounted on canvas, 459 x 2356mm. Yale Center for British Art, Paul Mellon Collection

p.12 Samuel Pepys, unknown artist, *c*.1665? Oil on canvas, 296 x 247. Private Collection

p.14 Samuel Pepys, Sir Godfrey Kneller, 1689. Oil on canvas, 762 x 635mm. © National Maritime Museum, Greenwich, London

p.18 Edward Montagu, 1st Earl of Sandwich, Sir Peter Lely, 1655–9. Oil on canvas, 762 x 635mm. © National Portrait Gallery, London (NPG 5488)

p.21 Edward Montagu, 1st Earl of Sandwich, after Sir Peter Lely, *c*.1660. Oil on canvas, 749 x 622mm. © National Portrait Gallery, London (NPG 609)

p.24 Sir William Coventry, John Riley, *c*.1680. Oil on canvas, 480 x 395mm. Reproduced by permission of the Marquess of Bath, Warminster, Wiltshire

p.27 Sir John Harman, studio of Sir Peter Lely, *c*.1666. Oil on canvas, 1245 x 1016mm. © National Portrait Gallery, London (NPG 1419)

p.28 Sir John Mennes, after Sir Anthony van Dyck, *c*.1640. Oil on canvas, 1080 x 876mm. © National Portrait Gallery, London (NPG 4097)

p.30 Frontispiece to 'The History of the Royal-Society of London' by Thomas Sprat (William Brouncker, 2nd Viscount Brouncker; King Charles II; Francis Bacon, 1st Viscount St Alban), Wenceslaus Hollar after John Evelyn, 1667. Etching, 226 x 186mm. © National Portrait Gallery, London (NPG D2945)

p.31 William, 2nd Viscount Brouncker, possibly after Sir Peter Lely, *c*.1674. Oil on canvas,

INDEX

Note: page numbers in **bold** refer to captions.